P9-DCH-817

OCTONAUTS ™

and the

UNDERSEA ERUPTION

GROSSET & DUNLAP
Published by the Penguin Group
Penguin Group (USA) LLC, 375 Hudson Street, New York, New York 10014, USA

USA | Canada | UK | Ireland | Australia | New Zealand | India | South Africa | China

penguin.com
A Penguin Random House Company

MEET THE CREW!

The daring crew of the Octopod are ready to embark on an exciting new mission!

INKLING
(Professor)

KWAZII
(Lieutenant)

PESO
(Medic)

BARNACLES
(Captain)

TWEAK
(Engineer)

SHELLINGTON
(Field Researcher)

DASHI
(Photographer)

TUNIP
(Ship's Cook)

EXPLORE . RESCUE . PROTECT

"There's a big volcano nearby," explained Dashi, "and it's about to erupt."

Peso gasped. He didn't know there could be volcanoes in the ocean!

"I'm worried about all the animals that live there." Barnacles frowned. **"Sound the Octoalert!"**

"Octonauts, to

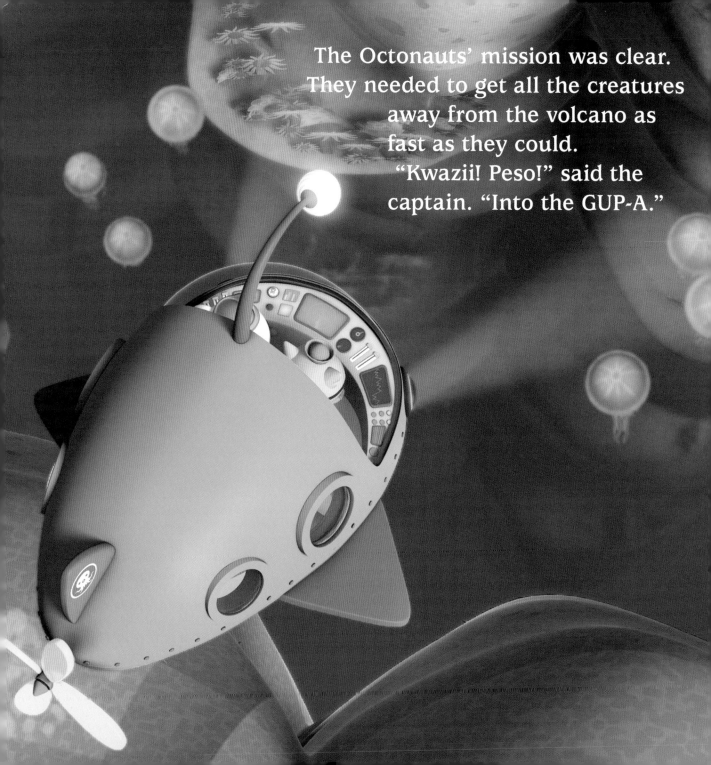

The Octonauts' mission was clear. They needed to get all the creatures away from the volcano as fast as they could.

"Kwazii! Peso!" said the captain. "Into the GUP-A."

The GUP-A dove down
into a deep ocean trench.
"Look!" cried Peso. "There it is!"
Shellington's voice came over
the radio. "Captain, the
volcano is getting hotter, and
the lava is rising," he warned.
"There isn't much time."

⧉ FACT: VOLCANOES

Hot lava and
steam build
up inside a
volcano before
it erupts.

Barnacles flicked on the GUP-A's loudspeaker.
"Attention, everyone!" he announced. "You must
all leave at once. The volcano is about to erupt."
Shoals of frightened fish flipped through the water,
but some creatures couldn't move that quickly. If they
were going to escape, the Octonauts needed to help.

First the crew put on their deep-sea suits. Next Barnacles gave Kwazii the octo-grabber.

"Use this to take care of the spiky creatures," he said.

Peso took a net to catch any slimy creatures. Barnacles made it his job to rescue any animals hidden in the rocks. No one would be left behind!

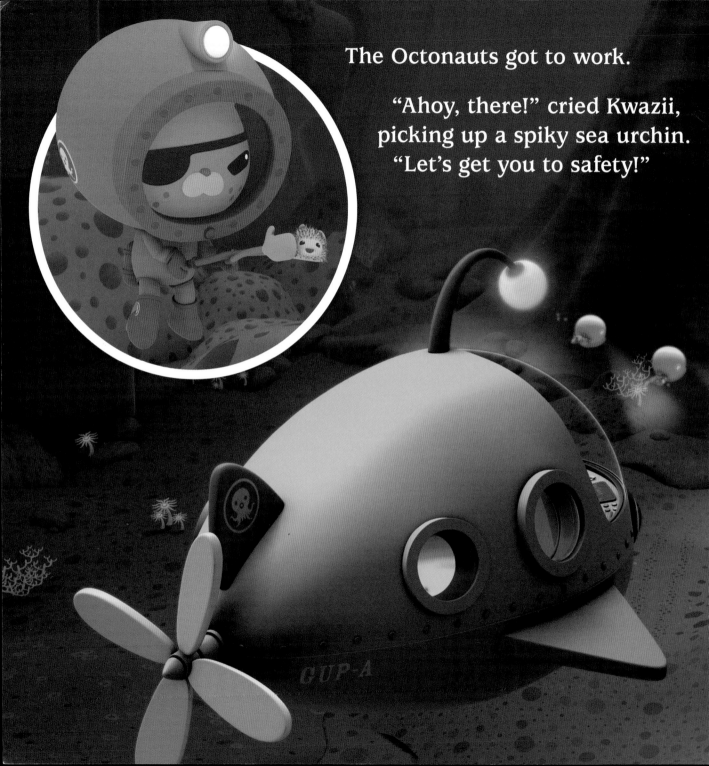

The Octonauts got to work.

"Ahoy, there!" cried Kwazii, picking up a spiky sea urchin. "Let's get you to safety!"

"There's a slimy one!" said Peso, netting a grateful sea cucumber.

Barnacles swam up to some stranded clams. "If you clams can't get off this rock, then I'll get this rock off the volcano!"

At the top of the volcano, Peso spotted a slimy pink fish floating in the hot bubbles and steam.

"Um . . . Excuse me . . . ," whispered the medic.

Suddenly the fish opened its mouth and gulped down a tiny piece of food.

"I'm Bob the blobfish." He grinned. "I've been waiting hours for my lunch to come."

⧊ FACT: BLOBFISH

Blobfish don't go after food. They wait for it to float past them.

"I'm sorry to interrupt your lunch," said Peso, "but this volcano is about to erupt!"

The blobfish shook his head. "I can't leave without my brothers, Bob and . . . Bob."

Before Peso could argue, a message buzzed in his diving helmet.

"We need your help!" said Kwazii. "Someone's hurt down here!"

"Go," said Bob. "Don't worry about me!"

Peso paddled down to Kwazii as fast as his flippers could carry him. It was his duty to help any creature that was hurt or sick!

"**Ooh!**" cried a poor octopus. Its tentacle was trapped under a rock.

Kwazii heaved the rock away, then Peso started bandaging. "Lean on me, matey!" Kwazii smiled. "We'll get you out of here in no time!"

"Shellington to Captain Barnacles!"
An urgent message was coming through from the Octopod!
"Please hurry," urged Shellington.
"The volcano will erupt in the next five minutes!"
"Got it!" replied the captain.
"Let's do one last check to make sure everyone's out."

On the way back to the GUP-A, Peso spotted
a worrying sight.
"Oh no!" he cried. "It's Bob, Bob, and . . . Bob!"
The three blobfish were floating right over the volcano!
"I thought I could get away by myself," sighed Bob. "But
my muscles are all jiggly like jelly."

There wasn't a second to lose. The volcano was ready to blow. "Octonauts!" shouted the captain. "Let's do this!" Peso took Bob, while Kwazii grabbed Bob. The last Bob was with Barnacles.

The volcano rumbled and shook. It was going to be a close one!

WWOOOSSHSHH!

The noise from the volcano was deafening. The Octonauts lifted the blobfish brothers into the GUP-A.
"Let's go!" ordered Barnacles.
Hot lava exploded behind the GUP-A as it powered away. They had just made it!

Back on the Octopod, the crew sat back to enjoy the display.
It wasn't every day that they got to see an undersea volcano!

"It's a good thing the Octonauts got us out of there."
Bob smiled.
His brother nodded. "It's so hard for us blobfish to travel."
"But now we're all on vacation together," their brother,
Bob, said with a grin. "Thanks, Peso."
Peso giggled. "No *blob-lem*!"

CAPTAIN'S LOG

Calling all Octonauts! Our mission to the undersea volcano introduced to us three fascinating fish—the blobfish brothers. These interesting fellows float in the murky depths waiting for food to drift by.

CAPTAIN BARNACLES

⊫ FACT FILE: THE BLOBFISH

OCTOFACTS

The blobfish can hardly swim at all—its muscles are too weak.

Its special body helps it to live comfortably in deep waters.

The blobfish is a rare sight, but it can be found in the ocean around Australia.

The blobfish is a real creature, even though it is mostly made out of jelly! Its wobbly body helps it to float in the water.

It lives in the Twilight Zone.

Its favorite food is not known.

EXPLORE . RESCUE . PROTECT